The Oregon Trail™

The text was set in Garamond.
The display text was set in Pixel-Western, Press Start 2P, and Slim Thin Pixelettes.
Illustrations by June Brigman, Yancey Labat, Ron Wagner, Hi-Fi Color Design, and
Walden Font Co.

ISBN: 978-1-328-55001-9 paper over board
ISBN: 978-1-328-54997-6 paperback

Printed in the United States of America
DOC 10 9 8 7 6 5 4 3 2
4500727015

The Oregon Trail™

DANGER AT THE HAUNTED GATE

by JESSE WILEY

Houghton Mifflin Harcourt
BOSTON NEW YORK

1850
Oregon City
OREGON
TERRITORY
Three Island Crossing
CALIFORNIA
UTAH
TERRITORY
NEW MEXIC
TERRITOR
Legend
Oregon Trail
TERRITORIES
State Lines (Modern Day)

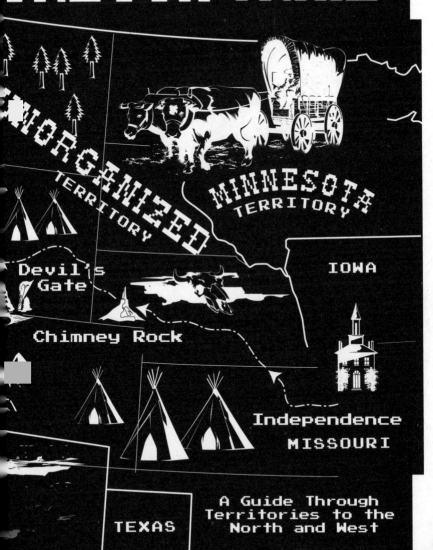

OREGON TRAIL

UNORGANIZED TERRITORY

MINNESOTA TERRITORY

Devil's Gate

IOWA

Chimney Rock

Independence

MISSOURI

TEXAS

A Guide Through
Territories to the
North and West

The Oregon Trail™

GO WEST
Live the Adventure

You are a young pioneer headed by wagon train to Oregon Territory in the year 1850. You've already traveled almost six hundred miles from Independence, Missouri, to Chimney Rock, in what is now Nebraska. You and your family are on the second leg of your journey across the wild frontier—and you're aiming to reach Devil's Gate, mysterious cliffs in what later becomes Wyoming. Once you get there, your journey West will be nearly half over.

For the last six weeks, you've walked beside your covered wagon for fifteen miles a day along the Oregon Trail. You can't ride inside, because your wagon is full of supplies for the long journey.

By the time you'd gotten to Chimney Rock, you'd braved river crossings, wild animal encounters, and disease. You'd learned to trade with merchants and Native American people, and also encountered snakes and bears. But that's only the start of your journey— and there are still months of adventures between you and Oregon.

Only one route will get you safely through this book to Devil's Gate, but there are twenty-two possible endings, full of near-victories, dangers, and surprises. Along the way, no matter what path you choose, you will experience natural disasters, unpredictable weather, sickness, and other hazards.

You're stuck in quicksand. How will you get out?

A tornado strikes! What can you do?

A herd of buffalo is stampeding your way!

Before you begin, make sure to read the *Guide to the Trail* at the back of the book, starting on page 154. It's filled with important information you'll need to make wise choices.

On the Trail, you'll get advice from friends, Native American people, or from Ma and Pa— but also trust your own judgment when you make decisions. Use the resources you have and you'll find your way to the haunted gate!

Will you survive?
It's in your hands!

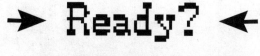

➔ Ready? ⬅

BLAZE A TRAIL TO THE

HAUNTED GATE!

Chimney Rock

JUNE 11, 1850

You hear the familiar blare of the morning bugle, which stirs you from a deep slumber.

"How can it be time to wake up already?" Samuel moans loudly.

"I feel like I just went to sleep," adds Hannah.

You tug a feather from your sleeping mat and tickle Hannah's nose. Your little sister sneezes as your kid brother giggles and rolls away. Samuel hurries out of the tent to avoid being tickled, too.

Your whole family is awake now, though it's barely light outside. You all know the routine. You'll help Ma build a fire to cook breakfast, while Pa takes down the tent and repacks your covered wagon. Samuel will milk the cow, and Hannah will help fill the heavy iron kettle with water for coffee.

"May I have another johnnycake?" you ask Ma when everyone sits around the campfire to eat. You're extra hungry since you didn't want much supper last night, and you know you have a long day of hiking beside the wagon ahead of you.

"Of course," says Ma, as she slides another patty onto your tin plate, along with a chunk of bacon. You sigh as you bite into the salty cured meat. You've been eating bacon almost every day for six weeks now. It used to be one of your favorite foods before your family started traveling along the Oregon Trail, but now you wish for a fresh tomato or a fried egg. Ma has noticed that you've been avoiding bacon lately, and she encourages you to eat it.

"You need to eat for strength, my love," she tells you with a smile.

You glance at the sunburned faces of your family and realize you must look the same as they do. You've traveled almost six hundred miles since you left Independence, Missouri, back in May.

The journey has been long, with fifteen miles of walking every day. You've learned to live with the pain of the blisters on your feet and the ache in your legs. The wagon is too full of stuff for you to ride in, so there's no choice but to keep hiking day after day.

The trip has been exciting, too. So far your wagon train has mostly crossed flat plains, but you've also seen some huge rock formations and gorgeous waterfalls. You've met Native American people from the Osage and Otoe-Missouria tribes, and even been face-to-face with a grizzly bear! The bear was more excitement than you wanted. Best of all, you've made friends with other kids in your wagon train. Eliza and Joseph, whose father Caleb is the wagon train captain, have been the most fun.

"Roll the wagons!" Caleb shouts.

You scramble to wipe your plate clean. Hannah runs to place the dishes in the wagon, while Ma throws dirt on the fire to put it out.

The first of the wagons starts to move, and Pa drives your oxen team to the middle of the line. You're glad you're not at the end today, where the dust from the other ten wagons is the worst. Sometimes it's so thick, you cough for hours.

It's a clear day, and you can still see Chimney

Rock in the distance behind you. The tall, pointy rock is just as impressive as the first time you spotted it, several days ago. Your family had a good time camping at its base, and you carved your name on the rock, like other pioneers did before you.

Best of all, Pa used his skills as a carpenter to build things for others on the Trail in exchange for a cow, which Hannah named Daisy. Now your wagon train has three cows, which provide fresh milk. Even better, Ma hung a small container of milk on the wagon yesterday. All the shaking and bumping of the wagon turned it into creamy butter, a real treat on your johnnycakes this morning.

"Guess what's coming up ahead?" Joseph says, as he falls into step next to you. You know that the mountainous part of the Trail is beginning, and you've been on the lookout for the next landmark.

"Scotts Bluff," you reply knowingly, since you've been studying Pa's guidebook.

"That's right," Joseph says. "But do you know how it got its name?"

"How?" you ask. Joseph is always full of information. When you first met him, you thought he was a know-it-all, so you didn't really like him. But you soon realized that he isn't a show-off. He's just really smart and helpful, and he likes to share what he knows.

"Scotts Bluff was named for Hiram Scott, a fur trapper," Joseph tells you.

"So?" you say. You know that fur trappers make money by trapping animals and selling their skins.

"Well, Scott got really sick out in the wilderness, and the other trappers he was with thought that since he was about to die anyway, they could just leave him alone and continue their trip without him. That was sixty miles from the bluff," Joseph says.

You shiver, remembering how you've passed lots of graves along the Trail. You know that the risks of your travels include disease and death, but it's something you don't let yourself think about too much.

Joseph continues: "Scott didn't die where the trappers left him, and he crawled all the way to the bluff. His bones were found there months later. That's why Scotts Bluff is named after him."

You stop for a minute, and make a face as you imagine that terrible journey.

"What does Scotts Bluff look like?"

"I don't know," replies Joseph. "But I heard it's not easy to get through."

That night, as you lay in your tent, you think about the scary story Joseph told you. You shiver under your warm blanket, grateful for the sounds of Samuel and Hannah's breathing beside you, because it soothes you to sleep.

The next afternoon, you see steep cliffs rising above the plains, and you know you have almost reached Scotts Bluff.

Caleb calls a wagon train meeting when you halt for the afternoon break. You listen quietly and chew on a piece of buffalo jerky, while the grown-ups talk.

"We have a choice," explains Caleb. "Either we try a shortcut through a gap in the cliffs, or we go the steadier, longer way around them."

"What is the disadvantage to going around them?" Pa asks.

"We'd lose a few days," says Caleb.

"And if we go through?" Ma asks.

"We should be able to make it in a day, but the route is dangerous and unknown. There is no map."

Everyone starts to debate. You've been rushing to try to get to Independence Rock for the big Fourth of

July celebration, and no one wants to delay. But will traveling through the bluffs be too difficult?

What do you decide to do?

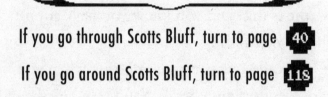

If you go through Scotts Bluff, turn to page **40**

If you go around Scotts Bluff, turn to page **118**

I think we should probably lighten the load on these animals," Pa says. You help him sort through the wagon to see what makes sense to leave behind. The decisions you make now will impact the rest of the trip, so Ma and Pa are being extra careful. The heaviest things in the wagon are Pa's tools, spare wagon parts, and the food.

"Based on how much we've been using, I think we can make it with half of this bacon, and less of this flour," Ma says, pointing to the fifty-pound sacks of flour. Pa nods in agreement.

"Bacon is only a penny a pound at trading posts and we're tired of eating it anyway," Ma adds. You think about the tons of bacon you've seen abandoned by other trailblazers along the way.

You help stack all of the things you are leaving behind in a pile.

Maybe someone else will come along and pick up something they need.

"Well, that does it. I think the oxen will start moving a bit faster," Pa declares. Over the next couple days, you notice that the lighter wagon doesn't seem to be helping. The oxen are moving even slower than before, and your wagon starts to lag behind the rest of the wagons.

"Let's stop for a rest," Ma says hopefully. But as you take a break, the oxen just sink to their knees. They never get up again. Now you don't know if you're going to keep going, either.

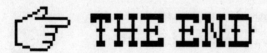 **THE END**

Mrs. Smith doesn't seem at all interested in eating, so you take the food and water from her. There's no point in letting the food go to waste, so you eat it before gulping down the water.

After eating and drinking, you play with the little boy for a while, until he finally gets tired enough to fall asleep. Meanwhile Mrs. Smith rocks the baby until she finally stops crying and falls asleep, and then Mrs. Smith herself falls asleep.

"Thank you so much for your kindness," Mr. Smith says, walking you back to your camp. "It really means a lot to us."

The next morning when you wake up, you feel cramps in your stomach, and wonder if it was something you ate. Could it have been the beans and bacon? Or maybe it was the water? You wonder where they filled their water barrel. You know not all families are as careful as Ma to always have clean water.

At first, you try to ignore the pain. But the next day, you get diarrhea, and it won't stop. You don't feel like eating, and you can't seem to keep any food down anyway. Over the next few days, you develop a fever and get weaker.

Finally, you collapse. You die of dysentery.

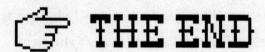 **THE END**

You run under the tree and huddle together. The rain is coming down in heavy sheets, and you and Eliza are getting soaked. Loud claps of thunder shake you to your core.

"Do you think we should stay here?" asks Eliza.

"Let's wait for a little while for the rain to calm down and then we'll make a run for it," you say. Eliza nods in agreement.

The thunder and lighting ease up after a few minutes, and you decide this is your chance. You grab Eliza's hand and run out from under the tree, but Eliza slips, and you both fall. You look out and see a bolt of lighting only a few feet away from you. Then thunder booms so hard you cover your ears.

"Let's go!" you yell, pulling Eliza up behind you. You run into the open field, your heart pounding. Camp is within sight when suddenly you are knocked to the ground by a tremendous force. You feel like you are spinning, and start to gag. You can't feel or move your legs at all. You try to open your eyes to look, but all you see is whiteness. You've always wondered what it would feel like to be struck by lightning. Now you know, but just long enough to realize it's even worse than you imagined.

 **THE END**

You see the dust cloud from the stampede growing in the distance, and the thunderous sound is getting louder. The ground beneath your feet starts to shake. Someone from a few wagons behind you shouts, "GO!"

Everyone scrambles, as if in a giant race. Today your family is at the back of the wagon train. As the commotion begins, Pa races back to you.

"Move! Quick!" he yells, throwing Hannah and Samuel into the wagon along with Archie.

Pa hollers at the oxen to move faster. All the wagons race at a frantic pace and shake violently as the herd approaches.

Archie jumps out of the wagon. Hannah tries to grab him and almost falls out after him. Your dog takes off, running faster than you can.

"Let him go," you pant. You grab Ma's hand as she stumbles over her skirt trying to keep up with you.

The buffalo are so close you can smell them. Their hooves are the loudest and scariest sound you have ever heard in your life. Suddenly, your wagon flips over and everything goes flying.

"Hannah! Samuel!" yells Ma.

You find your brother and sister in a pile of your things. The wagon wheels are still spinning next to them. You cover them with your body and close your eyes as the stampeding herd heads straight for you. You brace yourself for the impact of the hooves and hope it is over quickly. This is not quite the wagon race you had in mind.

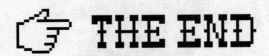 **THE END**

You head over to the fort the next morning with Pa to look for George. Pa is leading Daisy, who your family has decided to trade for the packing mules. You've also got a few of Pa's extra tools and a saddle you don't really need.

George gets up from the table where he's sitting with some other traders. There are mugs of coffee on the table and some johnnycakes, which he offers you.

"No, thank you," Pa says. "We've had our morning meal."

"Let's see what you have for me," George says. He rummages through Pa's tools and inspects the saddle. Finally he stops and turns to Pa.

"It's a deal."

George shakes hands with Pa and goes around

to the side of the building, leading Daisy away. You feel a pang of sadness as you watch the cow leave. No more fresh milk and butter for your family, and no more cream, either.

A few moments later George returns with the two packing mules. They are a little smaller than you had expected, but George presents them proudly.

"Look at these beauties," he says with a flourish. "These creatures can carry about two hundred pounds of load each."

You help Pa lead the animals back to camp. He and Ma repack the wagon to make it lighter and load several hundred pounds onto the mules.

"This should help us move faster," Pa says, looking satisfied.

Over the next few days, you do travel at a good pace. The lighter wagon is easier to get over the rocky terrain, and the oxen aren't as exhausted as they were before. But eventually, you notice that the mules seem to be getting weaker, and they start to move slower and slower. About five days after you've gotten them, one finally sits down and just refuses to get up. A few minutes later, the second one follows.

"What's the matter with them?" you ask Pa.

"I don't know," he says, looking worried. The mules start to roll around on the ground as you watch, confused.

Pa runs to get the vet who is on your wagon train. He examines the mules carefully.

"I'm afraid these animals have colic," he says.

"Like when babies cry a lot?" you ask.

"No, much worse," the vet says. "It looks like their guts are so swollen with gas that their intestines are twisted. You would need to operate immediately to save these animals."

You know that operating in the wilderness is impossible. The mules will have to be left to die.

"We were tricked," Pa says, shaking his head

sadly. "I think George knew he was giving us sick animals."

"We can't take that!" Ma says, furious. "Let's go to Fort Laramie and demand our cow back."

Going back means leaving the wagon train and having to catch up with it later. Pa doesn't want to waste the time, but Ma is insisting.

Will you agree with Pa or Ma?

If you go back to the trading post, turn to page **43**

If you continue on the Trail, turn to page **93**

I think we should go back to camp and wait for them there," you say, avoiding meeting Joseph's eye. You know he'll be disappointed that you disagreed with him. But you don't want to chase after Pa and the rest of the hunters. It might be dangerous, and you could get in trouble for disobeying.

You walk back to camp carrying the berries that you collected. Ma smiles when she takes them from you.

"This will make a nice pie," she says.

Soon, Pa and the other men return. They happily present their catch: five foxes and an antelope.

"I hunted one of the foxes myself," Pa tells you, looking proud, when you ask him. "It should fetch us a good price at Fort Laramie."

As you resume walking toward the fort over the next few days, everyone is excited. Ma can't wait to see a building after so many days on the Trail, and she's looking forward to stocking up on supplies. You're curious to see the nearby Cheyenne settlement you've heard so much about, and Pa has promised to get all of you some brown sugar candy.

When you arrive, you see a white building with a flag flying over it. The lawns are filled with wagons and pioneers, some of whom have traveled even farther than you to get here.

Pa finds the fur trappers and becomes instantly friendly with them. He learns that he can get even more money than he expected for the fox furs. The next day, Pa tells you and Ma that he wants you all to camp here for a while. That way, he can go hunting again.

"We'll make a fortune trading furs," he says. "We can save up a lot of money for when we get to Oregon."

The days turn into weeks, and soon Pa builds you a log cabin near the fort. You aren't going anywhere for a while. But luckily there's enough excitement at the fort to keep you busy and happy. It's a good life, even if it isn't Oregon.

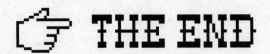 **THE END**

You help Pa pour grain from a burlap bag in the wagon into a bucket. Then you hold the bucket in front of the oxen and let them feed one at a time.

"Eat up," you say, gently stroking the coat of the poor animals. You hope feeding them works to counter any harmful effects of the alkaline poisoning.

The next morning you notice that the oxen seem a bit droopy, and their heads and ears hang lower than usual. Luckily, they still move without any problem and pull the wagon all day. It's been slower going on the Trail in general over the past few weeks. Instead of the fifteen miles a day you were covering at the start of the journey, you're lucky if you can make twelve miles over the rocky path now.

Over the next couple days, the oxen get sluggish and they start to lose weight. Pa doesn't want to drive them any farther. Instead you stay camped for a few days to give them plenty of rest and grazing time. It doesn't help. The oxen simply aren't interested in eating.

"Come on, just eat a little bit," Pa pleads with them as if they are little children. Soon, the oxen start to tremble, and you wonder if something is wrong with their muscles. Finally, they just give up and lay down on the ground. No amount of coaxing can get them up again.

You're stranded by the side of Sweetwater River with no oxen team to pull your wagon. You'll make camp for as long as your supplies last and try to hitch a ride home with some go-backers if you can. Turns out there's nothing *sweet* at all about that.

 **THE END**

You stay quiet as Caleb and Pa go over the rules and schedule of the wagon train with the men. Maybe after hearing stories of swindlers and thieves taking advantage of people on the Trail, your imagination is getting the better of you.

Even so, you can't help but think you see one of the men smirk after he and Pa finish talking about the man's new duties. The strangers hurry away, before returning with their horses, bags, and bedrolls.

Over the next couple of days, you notice the men don't interact much with the rest of the people in your wagon train. Instead they keep to themselves for most of the day, only coming around when meals are being served. They do accept invitations to supper, but after eating, they quickly head back to their own tent, where you can sometimes hear them talking in low voices.

"Ma, I don't think these new people like us," you say on the third morning.

"Hush," Ma says, looking around. "Why would you say that?"

"They don't talk to any of us," you say.

"Maybe they are just used to being on their own," Ma says. "It takes time for some people to warm up to new people."

You don't add that the men haven't gone hunting once since they joined you. Maybe Ma also wonders when they are going to make good on their promises to supply the wagon train with plenty of fresh food.

One of the men, who says his name is Nate, does take a liking to Archie. You see him call your dog over and scratch him behind the ears. You don't know why, but you feel a little jealous. You resist the urge to call Archie away from him, and tell yourself not to be silly. Maybe Nate is better with dogs than with other people. What's wrong with someone being friendly to Archie?

The next morning, when you wake up, the men's tent is quiet. The bugle has long sounded, and everyone is busy making breakfast. You think they must have overslept, and you remember how they agreed to pitch in when they joined the wagon train.

You go straight over to the tent to wake them up. You look inside and gasp.

They are gone! And so are all of their things.

You rush back to tell Ma and Pa.

At your wagon, Pa is making a discovery of his own. "We've been robbed!" he shouts. His gunpowder is gone, along with the sugar, and so is Ma's treasured jewelry box. The worst part is that all of the money

your family had left was hidden inside the jewelry box, so now it's gone, too.

"I thought something didn't feel right!" Pa says, wringing his hands. "We never should have trusted those men."

Everyone in the wagon train starts to argue with each other about why they agreed to let the strangers join. "They took advantage of us by saying they were hunters," says Caleb. "They know all pioneers are tired of eating beans and bacon."

Some want to send out a search party to look for the men. Others want to go back to Independence Rock to see if you can get some clues about who the men are and where you might find them.

If you search for the men, turn to page **95**

If you go back to Independence Rock, turn to page **106**

Your wagon train chooses to go through Scotts Bluff to save time. Every day that's saved means you're one day closer to Oregon, and have less chance of getting stuck in the mountains during the heavy snows. Your wagon train will go through what is known as Mitchell Pass, a narrow gap in the bluffs with two large cliffs on either side.

You look up at the jagged cliffs. They look like someone cut them out with a sharp knife. At first, going through the pass seems like a good idea. It looks like you'll be through it in just a day, as Caleb predicted. But soon enough you realize why people choose to take the extra time to head away from the North Platte River and go around Scotts Bluff. The narrow pass is treacherous and uneven. The oxen slip on the rocks. Your wagon wheels cut into the soft sandstone of the bluff, in some places leaving ruts more than a foot deep.

You keep pushing along slowly and steadily, until your wagon gets stuck in the soft ground. Pa tries to coax the wheels out by wiggling them, but your wagon is firmly lodged.

"I'm going to try to push the wagon, while you drive the oxen," Pa says to Ma. He braces himself against the back of the wagon and pushes with all his might. You and Ma help to steer the oxen. It looks like it's going to work, until . . .

CRACK!

You hear a sickening sound, which you know can only be one thing: an axle breaking.

There's nowhere to get a replacement axle where you are, far from a fort or trading post. Pa could try to build one out of a sturdy tree, using his carpentry skills. You'll have to look around to find a tree that might do the trick, but there aren't many around here.

"I'll do the best I can to make something," Pa says. "But I don't have all of the tools I need."

"What if you turn the wagon into a two-wheeled cart?" Ma suggests. She'd read about people doing that when they were desperate. "Although we would need to give some of the others our extra things to carry for us."

Ma and Pa debate whether you should ask for such a big favor, or just try to manage on your own.

What does your family decide?

If you decide to build an axle, turn to page **75**

If you create a two-wheeled cart, turn to page **108**

Do you think going back to the fort is a good idea?" Samuel asks you. It's been a day since Pa agreed to return to the fort to demand that George give you your cow back. He and Ma are convinced that the trader had known that the mules were unhealthy.

"Why, Sam?" you ask.

"That George man seemed a little mean," Samuel says, his eyes wider than usual.

You think about what he says. Something about George's manner did make you uneasy, too. He was a little too loud and full of himself for your liking. But after Pa's original concern about losing time on the Trail, he agreed with Ma that the cow was too big a loss to ignore. You split off from the rest of the wagon train, promising to catch up to them later.

When you finally arrive back at Fort Laramie, Pa goes to look for George while you help Ma set up camp. He comes back after a little while, shaking his head.

"Did you find him?" Ma asks.

"No, he went out hunting for furs," Pa says. "But I asked his friends to tell him to come over here when he gets back."

Later that night, you're starting to drift off to sleep in your tent when you hear loud voices outside.

"I'm not doing any such thing!" an angry man is saying. You recognize that it's George, and your heart starts to beat faster.

"But it's only fair," Pa tries to reason.

"A deal is a deal," George snorts. "You're the one who mistreated the mules after our trade, so why are you suggesting that should be *my* problem?"

"We did no such thing!" Ma says, sounding insulted. "They were sick when we got them, and you knew that!"

"You can't prove anything," George growls. You hear stirring in your tent and feel Samuel's hand on your back.

"I'm scared," he says. "What's happening?"

"Shhh," you say, wanting to hear.

"Now listen here," Pa says, trying to smooth things over.

"I'm not listening to any more of this," George says, getting louder. "Now you'd best get on out of here before there's trouble."

You don't hear any more talking, so you poke your head out of the tent. George has left, and Ma is crying. Pa looks angry but resigned.

The next morning Ma's crying has turned to wails. The oxen are gone, too! Pa runs to find George, but he and his trader friends have all vanished, and it looks like they robbed you first.

You never should have left the wagon train to come back, and now you're stuck with no way to return. Talk about a bad deal.

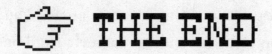 **THE END**

You decide to make camp along the banks of the little stream. The oxen eagerly chew on the yellowish grass lining the stream and drink the cool water.

Ma asks you to fetch water for the kettle, which you get from the stream. You set it to boil and add coffee to it. You never thought you would drink as much coffee as you have been drinking on the Trail. Before you started, you thought it tasted terrible and was just for grown-ups. But since you've been on this journey, the water you've gotten has often been even worse than the taste of coffee. With a little sugar you've learned to enjoy the steamy hot drink, especially after a long day of hiking.

After supper you pour the coffee into mugs and hand one to Pa first.

"Bleh!" he says, spitting the drink out. "This is really bitter!"

Ma sniffs her coffee and makes a face.

"Yes, this is really awful. What was in that kettle?" she asks you.

"Nothing," you say, confused. "I rinsed it out in the stream and filled it with clean water."

Pa's eyes grow wide. "I wonder if this is alkaline water! I've heard of it, but didn't know how to recognize it. It can be really harmful to drink, even for the animals."

He rushes over to talk to Caleb. The two walk over to the stream and taste the water. As feared, it is bitter and foul tasting.

"What do we do now?" Pa asks. "The animals have all drunk their fill of this poisonous water."

Archie! You panic when you suddenly realize that your dog could have drunk from the stream as well.

"Have you seen Archie around?" you ask Hannah and Samuel.

The three of you search and finally find Archie napping in the wagon, where he has been since you stopped for camp. *Phew!* He hasn't had a chance to drink from the stream yet. You tie him to the wagon wheel with a rope so he doesn't go near the water.

You head back over to Ma and Pa. They are trying

to figure out what to do for the oxen. The animals look fine for now, but they could get very sick soon.

"I think we should give them some grain from the emergency feed we have," Pa suggests. "It'll put something else in their stomachs."

"How about if we make them a mixture of vinegar and flour to drink? Maybe that will take away the effects of the poison," Ma says.

Which do you do?

If you give them the grain, turn to page **33**

If you give them the vinegar mixture, turn to page **131**

Pa throws ropes around the yokes of the oxen, working quickly. Then everyone grabs hold and pulls the animals forward.

"Keep pulling!" Pa shouts. "I'm afraid we might be in quicksand."

Quicksand! You've heard stories of teams of oxen perishing in a river by getting stuck in the soft sand. And even of entire wagonloads of goods being destroyed in the water.

Your heart beats faster as you pull on Daisy.

"Come on, Daisy," you plead. She cooperates and comes with you. You look back at Pa and the wagon, which is still in the same spot. The oxen haven't moved an inch.

"Heyaaa!" Pa yells, pulling with all his might. Finally, the oxen start moving again. Slowly the wagon starts rolling forward. You see Pa's face start to relax and you let yourself breathe. Your team makes it safely across to the other bank of the river.

"You did it, Pa!" you say. You watch as the other wagons make their way across, too, one at a time.

You try to dry off and drape a blanket around your shoulders. Then you, Hannah, and Samuel unyoke the oxen and lead them to a patch of grass to graze.

"Poor animals," you say in a soothing voice as you pat them gently.

You head back to the river. Pa and Caleb are helping the last family in the wagon train to get on shore. Pa holds his hand out to help the woman onto the bank. You see her clutching her baby, and feel sorry for her as she stumbles.

The Smith family has two kids, a little boy who is three and a baby girl. The baby is crying loudly as the mother tries to soothe her. But she herself looks weak, as if even standing up is hard for her. You wonder if she has been eating and sleeping enough.

Caleb takes one look at everyone and decides that you should probably end the day early. There is

still enough daylight to hike for a couple hours, but everyone needs to rest, including the animals.

As you start to make camp, you can't help but look over at the Smiths. The little boy is crying now, too, and Mrs. Smith is trying to calm him down as well. She jiggles the baby on her hip and tries to get the boy to sit down. But he just clings to her legs. Mr. Smith is rummaging for firewood and trying to build a fire as quickly as he can.

You look around to see if anyone else notices.

But everyone is busy setting up their own camp and doing their own chores. You help Pa assemble your tents, while Ma starts to make supper. Your family looks tired, too, but no one looks as worn out as Mrs. Smith.

Pa sees you glancing over at the family again.

"I can manage this on my own if you want to go over there and give the Smiths a hand," he says to you.

You nod.

As you walk over to the Smiths, you see the baby continuing to cry and the little boy still fussing. Mr. Smith has gotten the fire started and is now trying to get a meal together for his family. You help him warm some bacon and beans, and then carry plates and drinks from their water barrel over to Mrs. Smith.

"I can hold the baby while you eat," you offer.

"Thank you," Mrs. Smith says. "You're very kind, but I'm not hungry, and I can manage. Why don't you drink some water and have a seat? Standing over the campfire must have been hot."

The heat has made you thirsty, and you'd like to stop and rest, but you came here to help. Do you push her to eat a little bit, or take the cup of water and sit down?

If you take the water, turn to page **21**

If you insist that Mrs. Smith eat a little, turn to page **87**

I'm scared for us to stay here all alone," you tell Ma. "Pa knows his way and can catch up with us on the Trail."

"I guess you're right," Ma says, barely able to fight back her tears. "Pa would want us to stay safe and stick with the others."

As you hike that day, you scan the area around you for any sign of Pa. But you don't see him, and you try to ignore the feeling of dread that grips your heart.

When you stop for the midday break, you hear a shout from nearby.

"They're back!" Caleb says.

You see an exhausted Pa coming toward you and race out to meet him. He opens his arms wide and gives you a tight hug.

"Where have you been?" you ask, as Ma, Samuel, and Hannah run to join you.

"We were looking for the men and followed their tracks for a while. And then we came across a wagon train that had lost half of their party to a mysterious illness." Pa's voice quivers as he speaks.

"Those that were left were weak and sick, and low on supplies, so we helped them hunt and helped them bury their dead," he continues. A cloud passes over his eyes, and you wonder what horrors he witnessed.

That night you can't sleep, even though you're so relieved to have Pa back. You come out of your tent and hear him talking to Ma.

"I don't want to be out here anymore," he is saying. "It's too dangerous. Let's go home."

Ma murmurs her agreement, and you know that it's final. You're going to be go-backers. And after hearing Pa's tales of the starving, dying wagon train, you're fine with that.

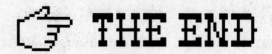 **THE END**

Excuse me, Pa," you interrupt. "Can I speak to you alone for a minute?" Pa looks at you with concern, and agrees.

"I think there is something unusual going on."

You take a deep breath and continue, carefully explaining everything you observed.

As you speak, a woman from a nearby tent runs over.

"Don't trust that man!" she shouts breathlessly as she points her finger to the man who has been talking to Caleb.

"He and his brothers are thieves." She leans on your wagon to catch her breath. "They robbed another wagon train last week!"

As the woman talks, the men suddenly hurry away without saying a word.

"There are good and bad people everywhere," the woman continues. "I'm afraid the Trail is no different. More than one group of thieves has come through while I've been camping here."

In the morning, as the wagons roll out, your family is near the back. You'll head along Sweetwater River now, and you'll have to cross the winding river at different points over and over.

After crossing a rocky patch following your midday break, you hear a faint rumble, like the sound of thunder. You look around, confused, because the skies are completely clear. Not another tornado, you hope!

You see Caleb search the horizon and turn.

"It's a stampede!" he yells. "Hundreds of buffalo must be headed our way!"

The rumbling gets louder as the animals barrel over fields and rocks toward you.

"What do we do?" Ma says. "We'll all be crushed to death!" Her eyes grow wide with fear.

"Let's outrun them," Pa says. "Hurry!"

"We can't! We'll have to scare them with fire," Caleb shouts.

"But isn't fire just as dangerous?" Ma asks. "What if it gets out of control?"

"The river and rocks will stop it," Caleb says. "Let's move!"

You look at Ma and Pa. Everyone has only a few seconds to decide. What do you do?

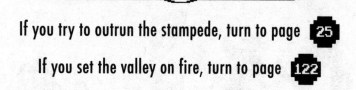

If you try to outrun the stampede, turn to page **25**

If you set the valley on fire, turn to page **122**

You're glad that Ma and Pa decide to keep the cow. You've gotten used to having a little bit of fresh milk and butter every day, and also cream sometimes as a treat. And you find the cow calming. Maybe it's the way Daisy chews her cud like nothing else in the world matters.

It's fun to be at the fort for a couple of days. You and the other kids organize a big game on the lawn. Everyone divides into two wagon teams. You take turns throwing buffalo chips to the other team to catch. If a team catches a chip, they get a point.

"Catch it!" Hannah shouts, her cheeks flushed from running, as a chip comes right at Samuel.

Samuel dives to catch the chip and comes up with it. Your wagon group cheers. You won!

When you aren't playing, you help Ma and Pa sort through the wagon. Pa is taking George's advice to unload any extra items. And Ma wants to make sure you stock up on things you are running out of, like salt and coffee. As Ma had feared, everything at the fort is very expensive. But she manages to get the things you need.

You leave the fort feeling rested and happy. You'll travel along the North Platte River for a while now. But you soon find that the journey is slower, just like George had warned. There are lots of boulders and rocks to travel over. Your wagon wheels get stuck from time to time, and everyone helps to clear the way.

You're traveling higher and higher as you get closer to the Rocky Mountains. The landscape is vastly different from the hard, dusty, dry plains you crossed over the past two months. More trees are a welcome change, and makes it easier to collect firewood for camp. But being higher also makes the air seem a little harder to breathe.

After a few days of hiking, you have to ford the river. By now, your wagon train has made several river crossings, and you have a set routine. Expert swimmers wade in alone to measure the depth of the water with sticks. Once they find an area shallow enough to cross, they also determine how strong the current is, and then they guide the wagon train across to the opposite bank.

"Let's tie up everything tight," Pa says as the swimmers check the river. You all help to prepare the wagon. The last thing you want is for your precious goods to start floating away. Hannah and Samuel climb into the wagon, while you prepare to wade to help drive the animals across the water.

Even though you have done it several times on the journey, every time you ford a river you feel nervous. You know there is the possibility of so many things going wrong. Luckily, the water seems calm today, and the banks of the other shore are within sight.

Pa drives the team of oxen into the water, and you follow behind with Daisy. Archie is a good swimmer and can make his way across the water and climb into the wagon when he needs to rest.

"Yow!" You brace yourself as the cold water soaks your legs and hits your waist. Then you carefully wade through the sandy bottom of the river, trying to avoid rocks and fallen branches.

Suddenly the oxen stop and start drinking in the middle of the river. Pa waits for a few seconds and then urges them to keep moving.

"Come on! Let's go!" he says, but the oxen refuse to stop drinking.

You stop with Daisy next to the still wagon. Water laps at the base of it.

"What's happening?" Ma says.

"The oxen won't move," Pa says, looking worried. "I tried to get them to drink before we entered the river."

Pa coaxes the oxen, and you try, too. But they don't budge.

"We can try to pull them out with ropes," Pa says.

"Or just let them drink for a minute," Ma suggests.

What do you all do?

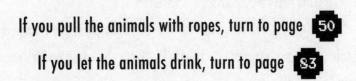

If you pull the animals with ropes, turn to page **50**

If you let the animals drink, turn to page **83**

The "go-backers" have you spooked, and your family is convinced that you should stay far away from Devil's Gate. Others, including Caleb, want to stay on the Trail, so the wagon train splits into two groups.

"We'll meet up with them on the other side," Pa says. He walks over to Caleb, and they exchange smiles and a firm handshake.

Pa takes on the role of wagon leader for your small group. He encourages everyone to head out extra early the next day. As you leave the Trail, you see the huge gaping hole in the rocks of Devil's Gate in the distance, and think about the legend. It's an amazing sight, but also a bit scary. You're grateful you decided not to go near it.

"I think we made the right decision," you say to Pa. He turns and gives you a warm smile. You've been traveling for a few hours when you reach the outer edge of Devil's Gate. Suddenly you hear a strange rumbling, and you notice that every time your wagon makes a noise, the rumbling gets a little bit louder.

Just then, the back wheels of the wagon in front of you roll over a large rock and make a huge thud. You look up and see rocks falling down the side of the cliff.

"Rock avalanche! Run, run!" you shout. Everyone abandons their wagons and starts running as fast they can. The chunks of rock come crashing down with incredible force and speed. Within a matter of seconds, you are buried.

 **THE END**

I think we should go find the hunters," you say. You imagine the disappointed look on Pa's face if he hears that they missed the chance to hunt the buffalo.

"I don't want to get in trouble," Eliza says. "You two can do what you want, but I'm going back to camp."

You watch Eliza walk away, and wonder if she's right, but it's too late now.

"I think they went that way," Joseph says, pointing to a patch of dense trees.

You walk together in the direction that Joseph pointed, while Archie runs a few paces ahead. Suddenly, something pops up from a hole in the ground in front of you. You catch a glimpse of a little face and tiny nose.

"What's that?" you say.

"A prairie dog," Joseph says. "I read that they live in burrows under the ground."

Archie starts barking wildly, and the prairie dog ducks its head back into the hole. Archie sticks his

nose in after it and tries to reach the squirrel-like animal, but it has vanished underground.

Just then, another prairie dog starts across the field nearby. In a flash, Archie takes off after it.

"Come back!" you shout.

"He'll come back," Joseph says. "Don't worry."

But Archie doesn't return, and as the minutes go by, you get more and more nervous.

"I'm going to go look for him," you tell Joseph. You set off in the direction Archie had gone, as Joseph follows right behind you.

The two of you call Archie's name, but you don't hear him. When you finally stop, you realize you have no idea where you are.

"I think we're lost," you say, feeling foolish. If you

hadn't run after Archie, you'd probably have found Pa by now.

"No. I think we're okay," Joseph says. "We just need to go back that way." He points behind you.

"That's not right, Joseph. I think we should try that way," you say, pointing the opposite way.

"That way is definitely wrong!" Joseph scolds.

You think Joseph is wrong but you don't know whether to just go along with him, or insist on going your way.

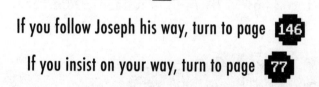

If you follow Joseph his way, turn to page **146**

If you insist on your way, turn to page **77**

You and Eliza rush back to camp, where you're happy to see that Pa has already set up your family's tent.

When the rain comes down harder, you are safely inside. You feel the tent shaking with the wind and hear the rain pelt its fabric. As the thunder booms, you hear Archie whimpering with fear under the wagon, and you wish he had taken shelter inside the tent with your family instead. He's always hated storms. You're glad that so far on the Trail you haven't faced too many of them. Samuel's and Hannah's

eyes are extra large as they wrap themselves in their blankets. You know they are scared, too.

You bury your face in your sleeping mat and wait for the storm to pass. It's a strong storm but it also ends up being a pretty short one. Soon the clouds break. It's dark and everything is soaked when you get out of the tent. Your stomach growls. It's late for supper and everyone scrambles to get things ready. Ma just needs to get a fire going. Then she can cook a stew with some onions and potatoes.

"How about some cornbread, too?" Ma asks you.

"That would be nice," you say. You eagerly help Ma whip up the batter. She'll cook the cornbread in a cast-iron skillet over the fire.

"There is still some butter left," Hannah says, peering into the container. Your mouth starts to water in anticipation of the warm cake-like bread with the sweet butter.

Ma looks around for a good spot to build the fire. Since everywhere is muddy and damp, she digs a little hole to find a dry spot. The few branches that you and Eliza were able to collect are too wet to use, so Ma pulls out some dried buffalo chips that she saves for times like this. Buffalo dung comes in handy when you can't find wood on the Trail.

Ma puts the buffalo chips into the hole, and Hannah hands her the bottle of matches, kept watertight with a cork. When Ma lights a match to get the fire started, the match just burns out. She tries two more times, but the buffalo dung won't ignite.

"How about trying some of these?" Samuel suggests, handing Ma a pile of leaves. But they are too damp.

You see everyone's faces fall. Like you, they are imagining a cold supper of prairie bread and dry beef jerky. It's nowhere near as satisfying as a hot meal.

You stand there looking at the hole, thinking about how hungry you are, when Archie comes and sits down at your side. You bend down to pet him, remembering that he needs to eat, too. You close your eyes for a second, thinking about what to do. Then you turn to Ma.

"Should I dig another hole?" you offer.

Ma shakes her head.

"I don't think it will help," she says. "We'd best get out the jerky."

Then you remember that Joseph once said that if you sprinkle a bit of gunpowder on fuel that won't light, you can get a fire going. Gunpowder is precious, and it's something Pa uses sparingly. But this seems like a good reason and time to use a little bit. If you can't get the fire going, the food you and Ma have prepared will go to waste.

You look around for Pa, but he has gone with a scout to assess the Trail ahead for tomorrow.

If you don't get the fire started soon, it will be prairie bread and cold jerky for sure. If you do get it started, you'll get to impress everyone with your quick thinking, and you'll get the meal you've been waiting for. Do you get the gunpowder pouch from the wagon and sprinkle some on the buffalo chips? Or do you get the jerky instead?

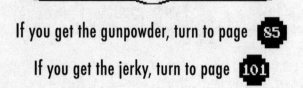

If you get the gunpowder, turn to page **85**

If you get the jerky, turn to page **101**

I'll go scout for a tree to make an axle," Pa says. "Do you want to come with me?" he asks you.

The two of you leave the rest of the family and hike toward a clump of trees. When you get there, you see that they are a lot smaller than they seemed from a distance. If anything, they are more like large bushes.

"We'll just have to make do," Pa says. "I'll try to make the axle as strong as possible."

Pa chops down the largest tree he can find and cuts off the smaller branches. You help him carry the trunk back to your wagon.

For the rest of the afternoon, Pa spends his time shaving the trunk to the right size and shaping it

into an axle. He has to remove the back wheels of the wagon and the broken axle. And then he has to fit it to the wagon and reattach the wheels.

"You did it!" Ma says, clapping her hands. "It looks as good as new."

Your wagon train makes its way carefully through the Pass again. You're walking alongside the wagon in your usual spot when . . .

SNAP! CRUNCH!

Your foot and ankle are crushed by the weight of the wagon. The axle was too weak and has broken again, but this time the wagon has landed on you. The pain is terrible, but what is really unbearable is the knowledge that your walking days on the Trail are over. You'll be riding in the back of a wagon to the next trading post, where your family will figure out how to manage now.

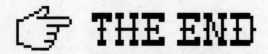 **THE END**

Fine! You go your way and I'll go mine," Joseph mutters angrily.

You stand there for a second reconsidering whether you made the right decision to split apart. Joseph walks away without looking back once.

You hear a faint bark in the distance behind you. Now you're feeling a bit more confident that you were right. You run quickly toward where you think the bark is coming from.

"Archie, come here, boy. Where are you? Come here, it's getting dark."

You hear whimpering sounds coming from a few feet in front of you.

"Archie, is that you, boy?" You speak softly, nervous about what you might find next. You move some brush out of the way and see Archie lying on his side, unable to move.

"What happened, boy?" You bend down and see a gash on Archie's stomach. His breathing is quick and shallow. Has he been attacked by something? You wish you had water with you to give him, or anything to make him more comfortable, because it's obvious that Archie is not going to last much longer.

Some wolves howl in the distance. Archie's ears perk up and he lifts his head to look around, and then, he is still.

Your eyes fill with tears, and you hug your dog for a long while. When you lift your head, you're scared. It's dark and you don't know which way to go. The howling grows closer, and the last thing you see is the shadow of an approaching wolf.

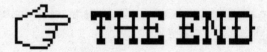 **THE END**

Your family decides to stay back, both because there's safety in numbers and because it just doesn't feel right to leave without the others. With everyone chipping in, more families will get back on the Trail sooner. After the Smiths, the last thing anyone wants to do is leave anyone else behind.

Pa puts his carpentry skills to good use repairing wagons. The familiar sound of his hammer makes you think of home. You organize the kids into a kind of game where you search for things that were blown away during the tornado. Everyone gets points for each thing they find, and the winner gets a prize. Hannah finds a bottle of matches hidden under a rock. Samuel manages to collect an entire set of spoons. Even Archie digs up a lost boot.

"Don't go too far!" Ma warns. She is busy sewing wagon canopies. Many of them, including yours, were badly damaged.

"I win!" Eliza shouts, pointing to the cast iron skillet and pots she found. You hand over the prize, a treasured piece of honey candy.

Your wagon train was lucky that no one was hurt during the tornado, apart from a few scrapes and cuts. One man got a big bump on his head where a heavy pan hit him, and some injured oxen won't be able to continue the journey, but it could have been much, much worse.

The buzz of everyone working together puts the camp in a better mood. That night, the fiddle comes out again. A man starts to sing "Oh! Susanna," and you all chime in. You feel good as you belt out the words.

"I come from Alabama with my banjo on my knee."

After a few days of recovery, everyone is ready to get moving again. You're going to follow the North Platte River and head toward Independence Rock. You never thought you'd think this, but you've kind of missed the routine of rolling the wagons each morning, breaking at midday, and camping at night. Your legs are fresh after the rest, and you're ready to stretch them again.

The day is clear and bright. As you walk beside the wagon, Archie runs along next to you. He seems happy to be back on the Trail, too, where he can explore again. He growls when he sees a deer. You catch a glimpse of it, a tremendous buck with big antlers. Then it runs away into the trees so fast it's like

it was never there. You know deer meat would have made a good dinner, but you're happy the amazing deer got away.

As you walk along the edge of a little stream, you notice the grass is yellow-reddish instead of green. It's sort of pretty, but it looks dry and you wonder if the animals will want to graze on it. Others have the same concern when you stop to make camp.

"This grass isn't green enough for the animals," someone says.

"I think it's fine, and we should camp here," another counters. "What if we don't see more grass tonight?"

What do you decide to do?

If you make camp here, turn to page **47**

If you look for another spot to camp, turn to page **134**

Pa decides that it won't hurt to let the oxen drink for a few minutes. You think about how hard these animals work, and wish they could get a proper rest. You put your hand on one of them and stroke his soft brown coat. But then you notice something odd. Either the oxen are shrinking or they are sinking!

"Pa, I think we are in quicksand!" you shout. Pa quickly realizes what's happening. This is the first time you've seen Pa use his whip, which he cracks loudly on the side of the wagon to spur on the oxen.

"I should have known. It's never a good idea to stop in a river," Pa says. He yells at the oxen to move.

"Let's go," he keeps repeating as he tries to drive the oxen. But it isn't working. With every second, it seems like they are sinking farther, along with the wagon. You try to help Pa pull the oxen forward by tugging on their yoke. But you keep slipping in the soft sand.

"Get the kids to the other side," Pa shouts to you and Ma. Water starts to rush into the wagon as you help the kids get to shore, and you see some of your things start to float away.

Caleb and some of the other men try to help get the oxen and the wagon out of the river. But it's not working. You see the disappointment in Pa's face as his dream of reaching Oregon slowly sinks away.

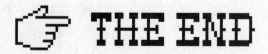 **THE END**

The idea of cold jerky is unappealing and you crave something warm to eat. You make your decision, and spring up.

"Where are you going in such a hurry?" Ma asks.

"To the wagon," you mumble. You jump into the back of the wagon and start shifting things around, looking for the pouch of gunpowder. Everyone will be so proud of you when you are the one who finally gets the fire going.

The only problem is that you can't find the gunpowder. You keep moving things from one side of the wagon to the other. In the background you hear Pa saying, "You almost got it," so he must have returned. At first you wonder if he's talking to you and encouraging you, but then you realize that he is helping Ma, who is still struggling with the matches.

Finally, you lift up a book and see the pouch underneath. You grab it and jump out of the wagon, and sprint to the campfire. Ma strikes a final match to try to light the dung, and as she does so you flip the pouch over and dump gunpowder onto the flame.

From the corner of your eye, you see Pa's jaw drop open.

"NO!" he yells.

There is a bright flash.

The next thing you remember is opening your eyes and lying on the ground. You see a raging fire for a moment, and everyone is running and yelling. Then you realize you can't move. You don't know it yet, but your arms and face are covered with serious burns. You will survive the injuries, but it is far too dangerous for you to continue on the Trail. Your family will have to turn back, as you see your Oregon dreams go up in smoke.

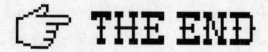 **THE END**

I think you should try to eat a little bit," you say. "And let me feed this little guy for you."

Mrs. Smith looks at you warmly.

"Could you?" she asks. "He hasn't been eating anything for the past couple days, and I have to feed the baby. But don't you need to have your supper?"

"I'll eat with my family in a bit," you say. "Hey, buddy." You beckon the little boy over to you.

"Do you want to play?" you ask.

The boy nods his head slightly.

You play a game where you throw a small rock back and forth, and every time the little boy drops it, he has to take a bite. Before he realizes it, he's eaten most of his supper. He laughs and claps, and by the end of the game he doesn't want you to leave.

"Thank you," Mr. Smith says, smiling. "You're really good with him. That is the most he has eaten in days."

"It was fun," you say, happy to see that the baby, now that she has eaten, has fallen asleep. Mrs. Smith is nodding off too, but you notice that she didn't eat much herself.

You put out the fire, then wipe off the dishes and clean off the skillet, and put them back in the Smith's wagon. The grateful look on Mr. Smith's face stays with you as you walk back to your family. You're glad you could help.

The next day, while everyone has breakfast, you notice Mr. Smith and the children near their wagon, but you don't see Mrs. Smith. "Ma, I wonder if something is wrong with Mrs. Smith," you say. "She wouldn't eat last night and she doesn't seem to be up yet this morning."

There's no doctor in your wagon train, but there is a man who trained as a vet. After your parents talk to Mr. Smith, the vet is called over to the Smith family's tent. After a few minutes, he comes out shaking his head.

"I'm afraid it's dysentery," he says. He lowers his

voice. "If she can't keep any food or water down, she could die. She'll have to rest here, possibly for several days. She may not get better."

"What can we do to help, Ma?" you ask.

"Let's each take a chore," Ma says.

"I'll pile firewood for them," Pa offers.

"And I'll make them some breakfast," Ma adds.

Caleb assembles all the families in the wagon train.

"We have to keep moving," he says, though his voice is filled with sadness. "We don't know how long Mrs. Smith will be sick, and we can't afford to wait. Hopefully she'll get better, and then they can catch up with us or join another wagon train."

You listen quietly. Caleb is right, but you wish with all your heart that Mrs. Smith gets well and that you'll see the family again.

As you hike that day, everyone is thinking of the Smiths. You cover the rocky path absent-mindedly and are surprised when Caleb calls time to halt the wagons for the midday break.

A little while later, you're sitting on a rock when suddenly the skies turn dark. It looks as if a cloud is falling out of the sky, and spinning.

"Take cover!" Caleb shouts.

You see the cloud hit the ground.

"Tornado!" someone shouts.

You watch, terrified, as the storm unfolds all around you.

Pebbles and dirt fly off the ground. The swirling

cloud gets bigger. Branches are ripped from the trees. The canopies of the wagons tear apart.

You look for a ditch or somewhere you can protect yourself from the wind, but don't see anything nearby. Suddenly, Ma pulls you underneath your wagon, where you huddle with your family. As it starts shaking, you can barely hear Ma scream, "Cover your heads!"

Then as quickly as it started, you see the cloud get sucked back into the sky. Everything is still, and your surroundings are eerily quiet now. The only sounds are of people crying and animals braying. You crawl out from under the wagon, and see all the damage. Several wagons are smashed to pieces, and some of the oxen have been injured, but, incredibly, no one has been seriously hurt.

Pa inspects your wagon. It's intact, although your canopy needs repairing. One of your sacks of flour has torn apart and there is flour everywhere. And some of your items have blown away. But, still, you're one of the lucky families.

Half of the wagon train is going to have to make major repairs. Some are going to have to decide if they can even go on. The rest, like your family, can push on and not get delayed further. You don't want to leave the others behind, but you have to think about what is best for your family.

What do you decide to do?

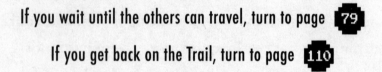

If you wait until the others can travel, turn to page **79**

If you get back on the Trail, turn to page **110**

Pa thinks going back to Fort Laramie is a terrible idea, and he refuses.

"At this point we would just lose more time," he says. The disappointment and shame in his face is unmistakable, and you know he feels terrible that your family was swindled. And that he was the one who made the decision to trade your cow for the mules. Even though she knows the trip is going to be more difficult without the mules and she hadn't wanted to trade for them, Ma goes to Pa and gives him a hug.

"Everything is going to be all right," she says. Pa gives her a grateful smile and walks over to the oxen. He puts a hand on them and pats them gently.

"At least we still have our trusty oxen," he says.

Caleb and the other men help Pa dig shallow graves for the mules. It takes a long time to bury them, so you don't end up hiking much today. Everyone is worn out from the ordeal and ready for an early camp.

That night, as you lie in your tent, you hear

coyotes howling. The sound always gives you the chills, but you find a way to force yourself to sleep. Soon after, you wake to the sound of loud growling. This time the coyotes are attacking your oxen!

Pa runs out of his tent and fires at the coyotes, and they run away scared, but the damage is already done. The oxen are seriously injured, and soon they are being buried alongside the mules. Your family is going to have to return to Fort Laramie now, carrying whatever you can on your backs, and figure out what to do next from there.

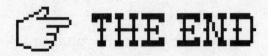 **THE END**

After going back and forth for a bit, everyone agrees to search for the men. Pa will lead the search.

"It's not going to be easy," Ma says. "Who knows where they are now!"

"Well, even though it won't be easy, hopefully this will be worth the time," Pa says. "If we get our money back, it certainly will be."

"Where are you going to look?" you ask. You figure the men could have taken off in any direction.

"We'll follow those tracks to start," Pa says, pointing to the ground. There are three pairs of faint footprints in the dirt.

After loading up on a breakfast of bacon, cornmeal hash, and hot coffee, Pa takes a bag that Ma has prepared for him with some prairie biscuits and buffalo jerky, a canteen of water, his compass, a blanket, and a lantern.

"We should be back in a few hours with the men and our belongings, if all goes well," he says. "But if we're delayed longer than today, keep going and we'll catch up." He gives Ma a kiss. Then he puts the bag over his shoulder and rides away on a borrowed horse, along with two other men on horses.

You help Ma clean up after breakfast, scraping plates and dumping coffee grounds out of the pot. And then you and the other kids get to play for a few precious hours. Joseph organizes the kids into a game of hide-and-seek. Ma pulls out her writing set to work on a letter to send to your aunt in New York when you get to the next trading post.

The day quickly flies by, but Pa and the others don't return by afternoon. As suppertime approaches, you can tell that Ma is worried, even though she tries to act like she is not. When night falls and they still haven't come back, your stomach twists with fear. What if something happened to Pa?

Morning arrives with no sign of them, and the day passes with Ma in a panic.

And now you are in a panic, too. By the next day, the rest of the wagon train wants to move on.

"I don't want to leave without Pa," Ma says to you, her face creased with worry. "Should we wait and catch up to the group later, or leave with them like Pa said we should?"

What do you think your family should do?

If you say you should wait for Pa, turn to page **126**

If you say you should leave with the wagon train, turn to page **55**

Get some extra plates," Ma says to you. You hurry back to the wagon and grab more dishes.

The three indigenous men get off their horses and walk toward your camp. As they approach you, Ma beckons them with a smile and points to the food.

"Welcome," she says. "Please join us."

The youngest of the men introduces himself as Little Wolf of the Cheyenne Nation. He thanks Ma, and the three men sit around the campfire and accept the plates of baked beans and corn fritters. When you finish eating, Ma gives you a nod, which you understand means to start making coffee for everyone. First you roast the coffee beans over the fire, then you grind them with the hand grinder and stir the coarse powder into the coffee kettle.

"Lots of bandits in this area," says Little Wolf after he finishes eating and takes a piping hot cup of coffee from you.

"We've heard stories," Pa says. "But we didn't

know whether to believe them or not. People make up all sorts of tales about the Trail."

"It is the truth," Little Wolf continues. "Where are the rest of your people?"

Pa looks sheepish. "We left without them after the tornado because they had to stay and fix their damaged wagons. It will take them some time to repair them."

"So few wagons means more attacks," says Little Wolf, shaking his head. "But we will protect you until they join you again."

Ma clasps her hands and smiles. "You're very kind," she says.

"What do you expect in return?" Pa asks, cautiously.

"We could use some gunpowder," Little Wolf says. "If you have it. Or sugar."

The next morning the Cheyenne men return as you are ready to get back on the Trail. They lead you on a path that takes you by their settlement, and you stop there for a midday break. Hannah and Samuel stare enviously at the children running around and playing.

Ma stops to admire a colorful woven blanket.

"How beautiful," Ma says. She convinces Pa to stay here for a few days. Ma says she can ask the Cheyenne people to learn how to weave during that time.

The days quickly turn into weeks. You make friends with the Cheyenne children and learn to love life on their land. Pa hunts and fishes with the other men, and your family realizes that the Cheyenne lifestyle suits you just fine. No one is in a hurry now to get to Oregon.

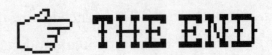 **THE END**

You get the jerky and the prairie bread from the wagon. Samuel pulls the tin plates out of the box they are kept in, and Ma starts to serve the food. Just then, Eliza comes over looking for you.

"We just got a nice fire going," she says. "Why don't you all come over and sit with us?"

Hannah jumps up first. "Hurray!" she cheers.

You take your plates to where Eliza's family has made camp. Ma carries over the stew and the cornbread, and soon the food is sizzling over the fire. As the scent of the food fills the air, everyone is in a much more cheerful mood.

The warmth of the fire has taken the chill out of your bones, and by now Pa has returned. You dip your bread into the gravy of the stew and take a big bite, grateful for the hot meal, and for good friends.

After everyone is done eating, Caleb pulls out his fiddle. Another man from the wagon train takes his harmonica out of his pocket. They start to play a cheery tune, and the rest of you clap along.

"May I have this dance?" Pa says, holding his hand out to Ma. He pulls her up and starts to twirl her around. She spins, laughing. Hannah and Samuel jump up and lock arms in a square dance. You grab hands with Eliza and Joseph and spin until you are dizzy. You all sleep well that night, exhausted but happy.

The next morning, you hike the rest of the way around Scotts Bluff. When you stop for your midday break, Caleb gathers the families together.

"Look over there," he says, pointing toward the horizon to the west. You can just make out faint purple shadows in the distance.

"Those are the mountains we will be crossing through," Caleb continues. "It's going to be difficult."

Everyone falls silent, thinking about what is ahead. You've had plenty of challenges already, but now that the prairie has given way to rougher ground, there will be different ones.

"But we are a hardy group, and I know we can do it," Caleb adds. You nod in agreement.

"We're coming up close to Fort Laramie," Caleb continues. You've heard of this fort before, and know it's a trading post that was built by a fur trader.

"It will be nice to be around civilization again," someone adds. "How long since we've seen a building?"

"And we can stock up on some supplies," Ma says. "I've almost run out of salt."

"I've heard that things are especially expensive at Fort Laramie," Caleb cautions. "The same items that cost five cents back in Independence can cost a full dollar there!"

Everyone starts talking at once about how people take advantage of the pioneers.

"It's like robbery!" one woman exclaims.

Then a man from another wagon pipes up with an idea. "We should hunt the foxes and antelope around here and then trade the furs for the items we need at the fort. I've heard we can fetch a pretty penny for furs."

"But it's already too late in the day to hunt," someone else says.

"We can camp here for a day or two," the man continues. He

looks around at everyone, trying to convince them of his plan.

"Isn't the fur trade slowing down in these parts?" someone else asks. "And we need to keep moving to get to Independence Rock on time."

"But wouldn't it be worth it, if we could stock up on all the things we need?" the man insists.

Everyone talks at once, arguing about whether to continue to the fort now or stop to make camp and hunt here.

"How about if the wagons that want to continue to the fort now go ahead," Pa suggests. "Those who want to hunt can follow in a day or two."

"That's a good idea," Caleb agrees. "What are you going to do?"

If you continue to the fort, turn to page **113**

If you camp and go hunting, turn to page **129**

Pa thinks it's a waste of time to search for the missing men.

"They have gotten a half a day's head start already, and we have no idea where they could have gotten to," he says to you all.

"So what should we do?" Ma asks.

"We should go back to Independence Rock," Pa says. "We can find out more about these men, wait for them to come back and surprise them!"

The feeling of arriving at Independence Rock is completely different this time. No one has any of the excitement you had before. Instead you're a little nervous about what is going to happen.

Independence Rock is still filled with loads of pioneers passing through. Everyone celebrates Independence Day here, even though the fourth of July has passed. You see people celebrate with feasts, flags, games, and even costumes. But no one in your group takes part in the merriment.

Pa looks around to see if the men are already back but all he finds are people with stories of how they were tricked and robbed, just like you. You set up camp and wait, hoping that the men will return. As the days go by, there are no signs of them. Maybe they have moved on to another site where they can take advantage of innocent pioneers, you finally decide.

"Now what will we do?" Ma says, hiding her tears.

Luckily you have a flash of inspiration. You see someone who doesn't know how to write his name pay someone else to carve his initials into Independence Rock. Before you know it, you are running a successful name-carving business of your own. You charge for both painting with axle grease and etching names into the granite.

At this rate, you'll earn the money you need to get back on the Trail. Eventually.

 **THE END**

Those trees don't look strong enough to build an axle from," Pa says, after taking a better look at them.

"I think we have no choice but to unload some of our things, then," Ma says. "Can you turn this wagon into a cart?"

Pa is confident he can. While Ma distributes your essential goods to different families, Pa works on the wagon. You can't help but be bitter that of everyone's wagon in the wagon train, yours is the one that has fallen apart. Quickly you realize that it's going to be impossible for anyone to sit in the new cart, which means even less rest.

"Maybe the cart will be easier to get through the mountains up ahead," Pa says to make you all feel better.

The cart does prove easier to navigate. But what is more difficult to handle is managing with less of your stuff and keeping track of who has it. You notice that the people you gave your things to start to use them, lose them, and eventually mix them up with their own things. Soon you are arguing over what is yours and what is theirs, and your back-and-forth becomes heated. Ma is really upset and tells Pa she doesn't want to continue like this.

"We can't make it all the way to Oregon without our own four-wheeled wagon," she says. Pa, looking defeated, pulls you and your little brother and sister together and breaks the news to you.

"We are going to stop in Fort Laramie and do what it takes to fix our wagon."

You know what this means. Your trip is on hold for now. For how long, you don't know.

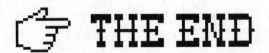 **THE END**

Your family decides to go ahead. Only four wagons are able to continue, and you count your blessings that yours is one of them. Unfortunately, Caleb's family is not with you, so Pa takes on the role of wagon leader.

Things go smoothly for the first day, but you realize that you don't have enough wagons to make a corral. That makes you nervous. You've heard too many stories of roving bandits and even packs of coyotes attacking pioneers on the Trail. You know most of the stories are exaggerated, but they're still scary.

"Do you think we should have waited for the others?" Hannah asks you as the day winds down.

"I don't know, but it's really lonely out here," you reply, looking around as the sun starts to set.

Ma overhears you and Hannah talking and confesses that she is a little worried, too. Somehow knowing how she feels makes you feel like you need to be extra brave.

"It'll be okay," you say aloud, trying hard to sound confident.

The worst part about leaving the rest of the group is how much you miss Joseph and Eliza. Now, during the rare times that you get to rest, you won't have them around to have fun with.

The day is almost over, and you are ready to make camp. You help Pa gather fuel for the fire, and Ma expertly gets it roaring. As you're sitting down to supper, you see some horses with riders heading toward you. Your heart starts to beat faster. Could these be bandits? As they get closer you can see they are Native American people. Possibly Cheyenne. Should you be wary?

Pa looks concerned, and he urges you and Ma to get back in the wagon.

"But we don't know what they want yet," Ma says.

"It's best to be prepared," Pa says. "I'm responsible for everyone now." You wonder if Pa has been feeling as insecure as the rest of you about being in a smaller wagon train.

Another man from your group interrupts.

"Should we tell them to turn back?" he says.

"No," Ma says. "Let's invite them to supper and see what happens."

Pa and the other man exchange looks as they consider that idea.

What do you decide?

If you challenge the Cheyenne men, turn to page **140**

If you invite the Cheyenne men to supper, turn to page **98**

After your family discusses the options, Pa tells Caleb that you will continue onward to Fort Laramie. Ma is eager to get there, and Pa doesn't want to take the extra time to hunt. He's confident that you can trade or buy the things you need, and he's determined to get to Independence Rock by the Fourth of July. You, Hannah, and Samuel are excited to get to the fort, too.

Caleb will come with you, along with most of the other families. Only three of the wagons decide to stay back and hunt for furs. They say they will catch up to you later.

You set off toward the fort, wondering what it will be like. When you arrive, you see Native people set up around it. Ma says they belong to the Arapaho tribe. You're impressed by their animal skins and feathered headpieces. They also have beautiful beaded moccasins and woven blankets set up for sale or to trade.

As your wagon pulls up closer to the building, you see soldiers in blue uniforms walking around. There are merchants and fur traders and plenty of other pioneer families, too.

"It's so nice to be here after so many days on the Trail," Ma says. Her eyes look wistful and you know she is thinking of home.

Later that evening, after your family makes camp, a confident-looking man approaches.

"Good evening," he says. "My name is George, and I'm a trader here at Fort Laramie. Welcome."

"Would you like to eat supper with us?" Ma offers, holding out an extra plate.

"No, thank you, ma'am," George replies. "But I would like to talk with you all for a bit."

"Of course," Pa says. "Have a seat."

George sits on the ground next to you. You're struck by how clean his clothes are compared to everyone who has been on the Trail for weeks. You feel a little embarrassed looking at how dusty and grimy everyone in your family is, but George doesn't seem to notice.

"You all have made a lot of progress on the Trail. Congratulations on making it so far."

"Thanks," Pa says.

"The Trail is going to get a lot harder from here on out, though, since you're getting near the Rockies," George goes on.

"Yes, we know," Pa replies.

"I can help you out," George continues. He looks around and points to your wagon. "You're far too overloaded and need to lighten your wagon to help your oxen drive through the mountains."

"What are you suggesting?" Ma asks.

"I'll take your extra goods and that cow of yours in exchange for two packing mules."

"Packing mules?" Ma asks. "Why do we need those?"

"When you get on the rocky terrain, they are

sure-footed and can carry a lot of supplies. Your wagon will be lighter that way."

"We've been managing so far without problems," Ma replies.

"But you'll soon see it gets harder to cover as much ground each day," George says. "The less heavy your wagon, the faster you can move. If you want to get to Oregon before the harsh snows, that will be important."

Pa has been nodding thoughtfully.

"But shouldn't we keep the cow?" he says. "She gives us milk and butter."

"Well, that's up to you folks to decide," George continues. "The mules are worth a lot, so I can't take less than the cow. Besides, you can't load the cow up with supplies, and she might have trouble getting through the mountains."

George says he'll be back in the morning, then he gets up and shakes hands with Pa. He tips his hat toward Ma and wishes you all a good night.

When he leaves, Ma and Pa talk about what to do. Ma wants to keep the cow, but Pa is tempted to get the mules. They discuss what extra items in the wagon they can get rid of and the things they want to get. You wonder what is the best thing to do.

What does your family decide?

If you trade the cow and extra goods for the mules, turn to page **27**

If you keep the cow and try to get what else you need, turn to page **60**

Most of the people in your wagon train agree that you should go around the bluffs, even if it will take an extra day or two. Preventing damage to the wagons is the safest course of action.

Caleb guides the wagons along the North Platte River, and you trek for a few hours longer. You can feel the stones on the rough path through the soles of your boots, which are wearing thin.

You wonder how your team of oxen, which have been so strong and faithful, must feel. Not only are they walking as far as you, but they also are pulling the loaded wagon every day. Luckily, there has been plenty of green grass for them to graze on every night.

"Woof! Woof!" Archie, your dog, sees a squirrel and barks.

"Hold on, boy!" you call out, afraid that he will chase the squirrel.

Archie has been great company on the journey, but he has also gotten you into trouble a couple of times. Last time he ran away, you ended up bumping into a bear while you were searching for him.

"Let me get it," Samuel says, ready with his slingshot.

Back home in Kentucky, you never would have imagined this, but your favorite dish on the Trail is "Brunswick Stew," which is made from squirrel meat. Samuel expertly fires his slingshot, and you smile as you realize you won't have to eat bacon again tonight.

"Halt the wagons," shouts Caleb.

You notice the clouds above getting darker. Caleb was smart to stop the wagons before the rain begins.

"I need you to go fetch some firewood in a hurry," Pa says to you. "And get it into the wagon to keep it dry."

"I'll go with you," says Eliza.

The two of you head toward some trees in the distance. You'll look for fallen branches and twigs.

"I can't wait until we finally get off the Trail," Eliza says as you go. "I miss sleeping in a bed."

"Me, too," you agree, "but Oregon Territory is still a long way away."

"I know. We aren't even halfway there," Eliza answers with a long sigh.

"We almost will be, once we reach Devil's Gate," you reply. "It means we'll have already traveled over eight hundred miles." You both pause as you think about what a huge distance that is.

"But it also means we'll have more than a thousand miles to go," sighs Eliza, looking down at her worn boots. "Sometimes I think we'll *never* get to Oregon."

"We'll get there," you say, sounding more sure of it than you feel. As you speak, the wind picks up and the sky suddenly gets dark.

"It's going to storm," Eliza says, looking a little worried.

You hurry to reach the trees, and start to collect branches that have fallen around the base. A few raindrops fall and you move as quickly as you can.

BOOM!

A flash of lightning lights up the sky. A loud clap of thunder makes you jump at the same moment.

"Let's get back to camp," you say. You hope the tents are set up already. It's no fun to spend the night soaked and shivering.

Eliza looks around. "Let's wait under this tree," she says. The tree offers a little shelter from the rain, which is falling harder now.

You pause, not sure if you should insist on going back to camp or agree to wait.

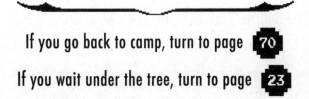

If you go back to camp, turn to page **70**

If you wait under the tree, turn to page **23**

Let's try the fire," Pa shouts. "I'm afraid we won't be fast enough to get out of their way."

You scurry to collect brush and make a line of it in the grass. Others get ready to ignite a blaze, and soon there is a roaring wall of flames. You feel the blast of heat against your face and hope it's enough to turn the buffalo away.

"Get moving! Drive these animals like never before!" Caleb says. "We still need to get far away."

Pa drives the oxen and your wagon jerks forward. The wheels creak as they bounce over the uneven ground. You run as fast as you can, until the muscles in your legs start to burn and your lungs feel like they'll burst. The dust cloud is thick and hard to see through.

"Keep going!" Pa yells over the thunder of hooves.

You run and run until you can't go another step. Then finally Caleb halts the wagons.

"I think . . . we . . . are . . . okay . . ." he gasps.

The buffalo herd has turned away from the fire. It looks like you escaped the crush of their powerful

bodies and hooves. You watch as the flames burn out, just as Caleb thought they would.

You're so relieved and exhausted, you fall to the ground and start to cry. Many others have tears in their eyes too, even Pa.

The oxen are sweating and spent. You give them water and set them loose to graze and rest. There will be no more hiking today.

"That was too close for comfort," Ma says, shivering as she thinks of what could have happened.

And then, you spot a wagon train headed in your direction. It's a bunch of "go-backers," pioneers who decided that they don't want to continue out West any longer. They are headed back East.

As they make camp near you, a few people wander over and talk to your family. They seem friendly and eager to chat.

Pa tells them about the stampede.

"We could hear it," one man says. "But we were far away."

"Enough of this Trail," a woman grumbles. "Stampedes, death, storms . . . I can't take any more."

"You've got Devil's Gate coming up ahead," the man continues with a grim face.

"Yes," Pa says. "What do you know of it?"

"Well, legend has it that a powerful evil spirit with huge tusks used to roam Sweetwater Valley," the man says. "When it was attacked by warriors, it ripped open the Earth and disappeared inside."

"That's just a legend," Ma says, "to explain how the rocks were formed. It's not real."

"But I've heard Devil's Gate is haunted," the woman replies, "and that many travelers have died there. I want no part of it!"

Now you shiver, as you remember the unsettling story from Scotts Bluff of the man who crawled there. You wonder if these are just scary stories, or if there's really something to fear.

Ma waves her hand, as if she is trying to dismiss the thought, but some of the others in the wagon train get frightened. After the stampede, they don't want any more danger. They argue for the wagon train to go far off the Trail to avoid Devil's Gate. Others think that it is silly to fear a legend, and they want to stay on the Trail.

What do you do?

If you continue to Devil's Gate, turn to page **148**

If you avoid crossing through Devil's Gate, turn to page **65**

We can't leave without Pa," you say, and Ma nods her head in agreement.

"I'm glad you agree," she says. "But that means we'll be out here on our own while the wagon train moves on without us."

"We'll be okay," you say, trying to sound more confident than you feel. "Pa will be back soon."

The next morning after the bugle sounds, you wake with the rest of the wagon train as usual. You do your morning chores and have breakfast, but when Caleb shouts for everyone to roll the wagons, you stay behind.

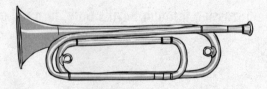

"We'll miss you," Eliza says as she prepares to leave with her family. "I hope your Pa gets back and you catch up to us soon."

"Me too," you say, blinking hard as you say good-bye to your friends. The past few days have been difficult on everyone in your family. Hannah and Samuel have been clinging to Ma. Even though Ma has been trying to look cheerful, her eyes were puffy and red this morning, and you think she must have cried all night.

You pass the day by reading and playing games with Hannah and Samuel. Ma works on the new quilt she has been sewing. Every time you hear a rustle or the slightest sound you stop and look up, hoping to see Pa. But it's only Archie or a squirrel.

That night, it gets cool, and you sit close to the campfire to warm your hands. You're staring absently

into the flames, when suddenly you hear the sound of hooves. It's a horse galloping toward your camp!

You look up at Ma, and she looks as nervous as you feel. But she wraps her fingers around a knife and stands tall as the rider approaches. As it gets closer, you see Pa's limp body tied to the back of the horse.

"Pa!" you shout, running toward him with Ma.

"Ma'am, I found your husband a few miles from here," the man says. "He was conscious but was attacked by a bear."

You gasp, afraid to see the shape Pa is in, but Ma doesn't flinch. She helps the man carry Pa off the horse and lay him down on a mat. Then she asks you to fetch some water so she can dress his wounds. Ma works hard to save Pa, but he never becomes conscious again. Ma is in a daze and hardly speaks after Pa dies. You've never felt more alone or scared as you realize you are truly on your own on the frontier now.

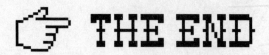 THE END

I'm going to hunt with the others," Pa says, after he and Ma talk it over. The hunting party will leave first thing in the morning in the hopes of catching foxes and maybe even an antelope or two.

"Can I come?" Joseph asks. Surprised, you look up. You've wanted to go hunting, too, just to watch, but have been too afraid to ask.

"Not this time, son," Caleb says. "It's dangerous."

The delay for the hunting means that you have a rare free day to explore. After your morning chores the next day, you, Joseph, and Eliza search the nearby area for wild berries and nuts.

"Let's climb up that big rock," Eliza suggests. "We'll get a really great view from up there." Sometimes you wonder if Eliza is part mountain goat, since she loves climbing and is really good at it.

You scramble up the rock, while carefully keeping your balance. When you get to the top, the view of the surrounding area is spectacular.

"Look!" Joseph gasps.

You turn your head and see that the valley is filled with a herd of at least a hundred buffalo.

"Wow," Eliza says. "Buffalo are even better for hunting than foxes."

"Let's go tell the hunters!" Joseph says excitedly.

"But didn't your father say it was dangerous?" you say.

"That was before we had something so important to tell them," Joseph argues.

"I don't know," Eliza says, looking worried. "I think we should just go back to camp."

"What do you think we should do?" Joseph asks, turning to look at you.

If you say you should find the hunters, turn to page **67**

If you say you should go back to camp, turn to page **31**

You help Ma mix vinegar and flour in a bucket, which becomes a thick, smelly paste.

"Let's add some clean water to it," Ma says, hoping that will make it easier for the animals to drink. Sometimes Ma has mixed vinegar with a little water, sugar, and citric acid to make a kind of lemonade for you, and it is surprisingly tasty.

"Here you go, drink up," she coaxes the oxen, holding the bucket in front of their noses, one at a time. They follow her orders and slurp up the mixture, and Ma looks relieved.

"Let's hope this helps them," she says.

Pa still wants to feed them some grain, so after they have their drink, he offers them some of that, too. The oxen nibble on it eagerly.

Over the next few days, your wagon train watches helplessly as several families' oxen die from alkaline poisoning. Thankfully, Ma's concoction worked to save yours. Others who gave their animals the same treatment share in your luck and are able to continue the trek. Those who lost teams, or with only half of their teams left, have to make hard decisions about continuing on or going back.

When you're only a couple days away from Independence Rock, your oxen start to move slower than usual.

"I don't know what's wrong with the oxen," Pa says. "I don't want to use the whip on them, but they are sluggish."

"Maybe the weight of the wagon is too much for them," Ma suggests. "The terrain is tougher now."

"Or maybe they need extra food," you add.

"They've been working so hard and have been through so much."

Pa looks at you and at Ma and thinks about what you both have said.

"We can lessen the load of the wagon some," he says. "But that means throwing away things that we might need later. If we give the animals extra time to rest and graze, we lose time. We need to save the grain for emergencies."

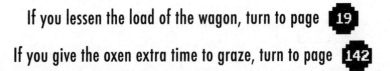

If you lessen the load of the wagon, turn to page **19**

If you give the oxen extra time to graze, turn to page **142**

Let's find another spot to camp," Pa says. "Look how yellow the grass is. This river is known for alkaline water, and it could make us sick."

You've heard of oxen getting poisoned by alkaline water, and you don't want to get sick either. You are a day away from Independence Rock, and you don't want anything to prevent you from getting there.

"What date is it?" you ask Ma. Lately the days have become a blur.

"It's the second," she says. "We're still on track to get to Independence Rock for the Fourth."

You've heard so much about that famous landmark. It was named by earlier pioneers on the Trail who reached it on Independence Day, and now you get to do the same.

The next afternoon you catch a glimpse of the enormous gray rock in the distance.

"It looks like a giant sleeping whale," Hannah says.

As you approach the formation, you see wagons and people camped in the fields around its base.

"The great desert register," Pa says. You've already carved your name into Courthouse and Chimney Rocks along the Trail, but everyone who passes through does this here. You will, too.

Everyone is giddy with excitement as you corral your wagons. Ma starts to prepare an extra special Fourth of July feast, working with some of the other families. You'll spend the next day celebrating how far you've come, as pioneers and as a nation.

You take a break from camp, and climb onto the lower parts of Independence Rock with Joseph and Eliza. It's smooth and shiny in spots. You look in amazement at the hundreds of names and dates

already written on it. Some names were written with axle grease and gunpowder. Others have been etched.

"Let's carve our names in so they never fade away," Joseph says, as he pulls out his pocketknife. You nod, wanting to leave your mark there forever.

The next morning you wake to the bugle playing "The Star-Spangled Banner." It's Independence Day!

You hurry to dress and gather with the others. Ma stayed up late last night sewing a flag out of scraps of red, white, and blue cloth. It flies on a makeshift flagpole in the middle of the circle.

The day is spent playing games and feasting on the delicious foods that Ma and the other women made.

Caleb announces a contest to see which kid can recite the entire Declaration of Independence. The winner gets a piece of chocolate.

"We mutually pledge to each other our Lives, our Fortunes and our sacred Honor." You carefully recall

each word. Everyone claps for you, and you win!
The sweet chocolate melts in your mouth. You
look around, stomach and heart full, as fiddles,
harmonicas, and banjos fill the air with the sounds of
celebration.

As you savor your chocolate, you spot three men
walking around the wagons while everyone is busy.
One of them peers into a wagon, and another looks
into a chest of tools. They don't take anything, and
after a few minutes, they leave.

Later, at bedtime, the strangers approach Caleb
and Pa. You hear one of them say that they want to
join your wagon train.

"But you don't have a wagon," Samuel blurts out,
which makes Pa look at him sternly, even though the
others laugh.

"That's right," the man says. "But we do have fine
horses, and we hunt and trap better than anyone else
on the Trail."

The man wears his hat low over his eyes and
doesn't look directly at anyone. Not being able to see
his eyes makes you uncomfortable.

"We can always use good hunters and trappers," Caleb says.

You see Caleb and Pa look at each other and smile. A few minutes later, Caleb and the man shake hands.

Then you realize something doesn't feel right. You think back to when the men were looking around your wagons. *Were they snooping? What if they're up to something bad?* You don't want to accuse anyone of anything, but maybe you should tell Pa and Caleb your feelings. Or should you just stay quiet and let the adults handle the situation? You don't want to make any enemies.

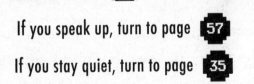

If you speak up, turn to page **57**

If you stay quiet, turn to page **35**

Let's be ready for anything," Pa says, while the other man nods. "Take cover in the wagon," Pa says to you kids and Ma. "Wait there until we know more."

You, Ma, Hannah, and Samuel hurry to the wagon. Ma lifts Hannah and Samuel inside, and you and Ma take cover underneath it. You peek through a wagon wheel to see what is going on.

The Cheyenne men ride all the way into your camp and dismount. There are three men, and one has feathers in his hair. Their faces look very serious, and you can't tell if they are friendly or not.

One of the men is carrying a large bag over his shoulder. He reaches inside, and you hear the sounds of rifles being cocked.

The man with the bag raises his arms slowly and shakes his head. The other two men follow his example and wave their hands as if to show that they are unarmed.

BANG!

A shot has been fired. It rips through the air and you hear someone fall.

"Pa!" you shout, running out from under the wagon.

"My leg!" Pa says, rolling around on the ground.

The Cheyenne men back away slowly, their hands still raised, and leave on their horses. The man from your wagon who fired the gun rushes forward.

"I didn't mean to! It just went off," he says, giving Ma a pleading look. "I was just trying to warn the horseback riders to stay away."

Pa survives the bullet wound, but his leg ends up infected. Soon he can't walk, and the infection gets so bad, it spreads throughout his body. Pa's trailblazing days are over. Ma won't continue without him, so it looks like your trailblazing days are over, too.

 **THE END**

Everyone agrees it's best to let the oxen graze longer and get extra rest. They have to work very hard to pull the wagons, and if they are unwell, forcing them to keep going can only make them weaker. It's a good decision, because after a few days the oxen seem to get their strength back.

The next morning, just as the wagon train is about to roll out, you feel a few drops of rain. Then it gets dark and windy fast, like it's going to storm.

"This doesn't look good," Pa says, staring at the sky. You look up and notice something different about it. Usually storm clouds are dark gray, but this time the sky is a weird combination of blue and green. And the clouds seem lower to the ground.

Just then, the wind picks up and the drops of rain now feel like pebbles. The ground is quickly covered with tiny white rocks.

"What is this?" you ask.

"It's hail," Pa says. You grab one of the pebbles and see that it's a piece of ice in the shape of a ball.

The pieces start to come down with tremendous

force, and as they hit the ground they bounce back up. Then the skies open up even more and millions of the pebble-size ice pieces start falling. Some of the hail bits are bigger, as big as buffalo chips, and they hurt as they strike you.

As you run toward your wagon to take cover, the wind picks up. Then suddenly the wagons start moving, pulled by the frightened oxen, who are being pelted by the hail and are running to get away from it.

"Halt!" Pa yells, racing after your wagon. But the oxen don't listen and keep running wild. Your wagon is shaking and things are falling out of the back and the animals start bumping into each other as they run. Suddenly your wagon flips over.

CRASH!

The oxen are tangled up in their yokes, and the wagon lies on its side.

A few minutes later, the hailstorm ends as quickly as it began. The sun comes out and the ice on the ground starts to melt away, along with your dreams of reaching Oregon. You feel a chill and wonder what you will do as Pa says your oxen team is seriously injured and too many wagons are destroyed to continue, all because of a hailstorm.

 **THE END**

Joseph starts walking away from you, and after you pause for a moment, you chase after him.

"Hold on. I'm coming with you," you say. You both know it's best to stick together.

Joseph doesn't turn to look at you and keeps walking, staring straight ahead. After a long, uncomfortable silence, you finally speak.

"It's almost dark. What do you think should we do?"

You look at Joseph and see his worried expression.

"I'm not sure," he says, kicking some dirt around with his feet. "To be honest, I don't know if we're going in the right direction anymore."

You look around, but it's too dark to make out landmarks and you have no idea where to go.

"Let's find a place to rest for now," you say. You walk a little farther, and now Joseph lets you lead. A minute later, you hear a howling sound.

"What was that?" Joseph asks. But you don't answer. You both know what it was: wolves. You just hope that they are far away from you.

"Let's stop here and wait for morning," you say, pointing to a cluster of rocks that form a shelter. You hope you'll be protected from whatever is out there.

You lie on the ground and close your eyes, but your mind keeps racing. *Where is Archie? Are you going to find your way? What are you going to eat?*

"Look what I found."

You rub your eyes and realize that it's light now. You must have fallen asleep. Joseph is standing over you with a handful of red berries in his hand. He gives you half, and you each devour your share.

Within a few seconds of eating the berries, you feel an intense burning in your mouth and then your tongue starts to swell. You're having a hard time breathing, and the last thing you see is Joseph's face turning the color of the berries.

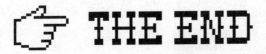 **THE END**

Our family will continue to Devil's Gate," Pa says decisively to the group.

"We haven't heard anything that convinces us it's a good idea to go off the Trail," adds Ma.

Some of the other pioneers are spooked enough to travel far around Devil's Gate, but the rest of you will follow a path that passes close to it. You're glad your parents feel so confident, because you're still a little nervous.

"Pa, I feel scared," Hannah confesses at bedtime. She clutches her doll as Pa tucks her blanket tightly around her.

"Everything will be fine," Pa says, patting her gently. "You don't need to worry."

"But Devil's Gate sounds like a terrible place," Samuel adds. "I don't want to go near it!"

Pa laughs a little.

"Devil's Gate is just a big rock, like Independence Rock," he says. "There's nothing terrible about it."

"Then why is everyone making such a big deal about it?" you ask.

"Sweetwater River cuts through the rock, making a gorge that looks unique, like a big gash, narrow at the bottom and wide at the top," Pa explains.

"But what about the stories?" you ask, not wanting to say much in front of your little brother and sister about Devil's Gate being haunted and dangerous.

"Those are just tall tales," Pa says. "As usual, we just have to be careful and smart, and we'll be fine."

Hannah smiles and tucks her tiny hand into Pa's big, rough palm.

"It'll be okay if you say so, Pa," she says.

"Yeah, I guess," Sam chimes in. Pa chuckles.

You murmur your agreement and drift off to sleep.

Devil's Gate isn't that far from Independence

Rock. Fleeing the stampede took you a little off-course, but soon you see the famous rock formation.

It sends a shiver down your spine as you imagine the evil monster from the legend ripping into the rock with its huge tusks. But then you have to admit, Devil's Gate is the most interesting rock shape you've seen so far. Once you stop being scared, it just takes your breath away, and you're glad when you camp early near the base to inspect it closer. As you expected, Eliza can't wait to get near it, too.

After setting up camp, you, Pa, Eliza, Joseph, and Caleb hike closer to get a better look at the massive gorge.

"I have a surprise for you," Caleb says, "if you're willing to hike for a while longer."

You all agree and end up walking for a few hours until Caleb suddenly kneels on the ground. He starts digging a hole while the rest of you look on, puzzled.

"Don't just stand there. Give me a hand," he says.

"Are we digging for buried treasure?" Pa jokes.

"Kind of," Caleb says with a laugh.

You all start digging, using the hand tools Caleb

brought in his bag. Soon there is a big hole a couple feet deep, and you hit something hard and cold, like a rock, but not quite.

"Is this . . . ice?" you ask, wondering how in the world it's possible.

"It sure is!" Caleb says, explaining that you are standing on a frozen lake that is buried underground, and in a few days, you'll come to an even bigger one called Ice Slough. You never knew anything like it was possible.

Everyone chips away at the frozen water and soon you have a cup full of the coldest, most refreshing ice you've ever tasted.

"When we get to Ice Slough, let's make sweet ice cream for everyone!" Eliza suggests. Everyone laughs at the idea of an ice cream party in the middle of the wilderness, and suddenly you're glad you didn't trade Daisy for mules.

You weren't sure you believed in miracles before, but you sure do now. It's too bad that the families who avoided Devil's Gate aren't with you to enjoy this special afternoon. But in a day or two, you'll meet up with them again and continue on the Trail.

As you suck on a piece of ice, you think about how far you've come since Chimney Rock, and about all the adventures and struggles your family has had. You survived them all with patience, persistence, common sense, and luck. As a pioneer, you escaped a stampede, conquered quicksand, and survived a tornado, just to name a few of the things you experienced, and you aren't afraid of scary stories anymore. You're also ready for the rest of your trip to Oregon. Who knows what other adventures and surprises are ahead on your incredible journey West!

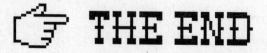 **THE END**

Devil's Gate
JULY 5, 1850

GUIDE
to the Trail

WESTWARD HO!

Congratulations on making it from Independence, Missouri, to Chimney Rock, in what is now Nebraska, on the Oregon Trail!

As you've already learned in your travels across the prairie, surviving the journey of a lifetime requires you to be careful and aware of your surroundings, and to make good decisions.

There's no substitute for being well prepared, so make sure to get all the information you need about what you will be facing ahead of time. This guide includes important facts about how to stay safe on the next leg of your trip across the rocky foothills leading to Devil's Gate, in today's Wyoming. Read up and then get rolling on the Trail!

DANGERS!

DISEASE

Cholera and dysentery come from contaminated food and water. Pioneers didn't know to boil water before drinking it. Drink coffee and your water will be boiled anyway.

FIRE

Stamp out campfires completely after use. If you encounter difficulty lighting a fire, do not use gunpowder as it is highly explosive. If foliage or fields catch on fire, rivers and rocks can be natural barriers to the spread of flames.

WILDLIFE

Watch out for coyotes, bears, and wolves. Coyotes are scavengers and dangerous to animals, but bears and wolves may attack both animals and people.

STAMPEDE

A buffalo stampede can be terrifying, and can't be outrun. Fire can steer the animals in another direction, but only light a fire in an extreme emergency as it can get out of control.

WEATHER

Take shelter from falling ice during hailstorms. In thunderstorms, nowhere on the Trail is safe from lightning, but the worst place to be is under a tree. If skies darken and winds suddenly pick up, a tornado can occur. Lie flat in a ditch and cover your head. Take cover from flying objects.

DISHONEST PEOPLE

Sometimes people take advantage of others on the Trail. Fort Laramie is known for dishonest traders. Trust your instincts.

POISONING

Never eat wild berries unless you know exactly what kind they are, as they can be poisonous. Identify alkaline water by looking for yellow-reddish grasses growing nearby. In case of accidental ingestion, a mixture of vinegar and flour can help stop the poisoning.

QUICKSAND

Check for quicksand before crossing a river by first sending strong swimmers to test the riverbed with sticks. Do not permit animals to stop to drink in the river during a crossing as the pause in travel could cause the wagon wheels to sink in the sand!

The legend of
DEVIL'S GATE

This mysterious chasm in the Rattlesnake Mountains has many legends around it. Some pioneers have died falling from the granite cliffs, leading superstitious travelers to believe Devil's Gate is haunted. They shiver and stay far away, avoiding the gap.

The legend says the break was formed by a powerful evil spirit. Warriors were fighting the beast, which used its giant tusks to rip open a gap in the mountain. The creature disappeared into the cliffs, and perhaps that is where it remains.

But these are just tall tales. Devil's Gate was created by the flow of the Sweetwater River, and it's not only safe to visit, it's one of the most impressive landmarks on the Oregon Trail. Don't miss it!

DEVIL'S GATE

THE Journey FROM Chimney Rock TO Devil's Gate

SWEETWATER RIVER

NORTH PLATTE RIVER

FORT LARAMIE

ICE SLOUGH

Devil's Gate

INDEPENDENCE ROCK

SCOTTS BLUFF

Chimney Rock

PLATTE RIVER

UNORGANIZED TERRITORY

Legend

Oregon Trail ⬅━━━
TERRITORIES ━━━━━
State Lines ━━━━━
(Modern Day)

☞ FINDING YOUR WAY

The Trail is 2,000 miles long (3,200 km) and there aren't roads or many signs, and the maps are not very precise. There aren't even states yet. The area between Missouri and Oregon is called "Unorganized Territory."

You are just one of 400,000 adventurous pioneers trekking West between 1841 and 1860. You have to navigate by compass and by landmarks mentioned in guidebooks, or by tips from other pioneers.

Remember, never leave the Trail or your group, and don't take shortcuts if you want to reach Oregon!

Look for these landmarks between Chimney Rock and Devil's Gate

DISTANCE FROM INDEPENDENCE, MISSOURI:

SCOTTS BLUFF: 596 miles (959 km)

FORT LARAMIE: 650 miles (1,046 km)

INDEPENDENCE ROCK: 815 miles (1,312 km)

DEVIL'S GATE: 820 miles (1,320 km)

The
Oregon
Trail™

LIVE
the adventure!

Do you have what it takes to make it all the way to Oregon City?

Look straight into the face of danger and dysentery!

Read all four books in this new choose-your-own-trail series!